To Cameron and Naomi with love. – OE

For Rodney and Sheila Pearce. – GM

SAMMY GOES FLYING
TAMARIND BOOKS 978 1 848 53050 8

Published in Great Britain by Tamarind Books,
a division of Random House Children's Books
A Random House Group Company

First published by André Deutsch Ltd 1990
This edition published 2011

1 3 5 7 9 10 8 6 4 2

Set in Bembo MT Schoolbook

TAMARIND BOOKS
61–63 Uxbridge Road, London, W5 5SA

www.**tamarindbooks**.co.uk
www.**kids**at**randomhouse**.co.uk

Addresses for companies within The Random House Group Limited can be found at:
www.randomhouse.co.uk/offices.htm
THE RANDOM HOUSE GROUP Limited Reg. No. 954009

A CIP catalogue record for this book is available from the British Library.

Printed and bound in China

Sammy Goes Flying

Odette Elliott

Illustrated by
Georgina McIntyre

Sammy wanted his brothers and sisters to come home.
He wanted to show them his lovely garage.

Then Jack, Jenna and Jess came back from school.
"Our school is going to an aeroplane museum. We will sit in old planes," said Jack.

"Can I come?" asked Sammy.
"No. You're not big enough!" everybody said.

"I don't care if I can't go!" said Sammy.
"I can fly to the moon. You can't.

I flew there with Teddy.
We saw the moon people and we danced with them.
You haven't seen the moon people, have you?"

"Last night we went flying over the trees!
We went on and on until we got to the sea.

We saw a lighthouse. Then we met some birds.
We did not sit on the waves with them because we did not want to get wet!"

"Then we came home
and went to bed."

"Stop talking about flying!" said Jack.
"You can't fly. You haven't got wings!"

"I use my arms, silly!" said Sammy.

"I want to fly!"
Sammy said
to Mummy at bedtime.

"I don't think they will go flying, Sammy.
They will just look at the planes in the museum," said Mummy.
"I've got an idea. We could go on a trip to see Grandma — just you and me and Daddy."

The next morning Jack, Jenna and Jess went off on their trip.

"Bye!" said Sammy.
"I'm going
to Grandma's!"

Sammy and Daddy and Mummy went on a train.

Grandma was waiting at the station.

"Hello, Sammy, I have a treat for you. A friend of mine
is doing something special at the sports field this afternoon.
I thought we could all go there after lunch," she said.

After lunch they all went to a huge sports field. It was crowded with people.
Towering above their heads was an enormous hot air balloon.

"Sammy, we are going flying!"
said Grandma.

"Are we, are we?" said Sammy.
"Teddy are you scared?"

Sammy, Teddy and Grandma climbed in.

Sammy held Teddy
very tight.
"Don't be afraid,
Teddy!" said Sammy.

Up and up and up they went, high into the sky.

Up and up and up they went until the buildings looked tiny.
   "There is my house," said Grandma.

"Teddy is not scared now," said Sammy.
"I love flying. Thank you, Grandma."

When they landed, the silky balloon
shivered and sank slowly to the ground.

"I went flying, Daddy!" said Sammy. "I'm going to tell Jack and Jenna and Jess! They said I was too small!"

"You can show them these when we get home," Daddy said.

"We saw lots of planes at the museum but we didn't fly," said Jack.

"I did! Look at these photos!" said Sammy.
"Daddy took them. I'm not too small to fly."

Jack, Jenna and Jess looked
and they were amazed!

OTHER TAMARIND TITLES

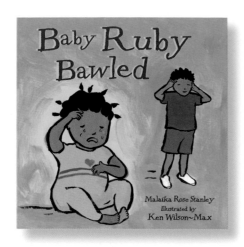

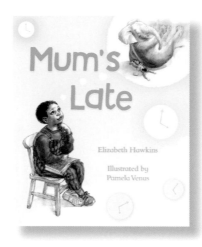

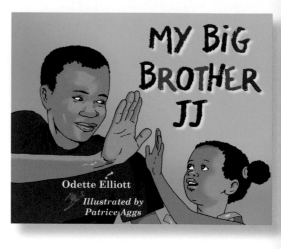

Baby Ruby Bawled
by Malaika Rose Stanley

Baby Ruby won't stop bawling.
Dad gives her a bath, Mum gives her
a feed, Nana takes her for a drive and
Grandad walks her round the garden.
But baby Ruby keeps on bawling.
Then her brother Theo has an idea,
but will it work?
Age 3+

Mum's Late
by Elizabeth Hawkins

It's going home time and all the
children are leaving. Except Jerome.
"Where's your Mum, Jerome?" asks
Mrs Stuart. Jerome doesn't know.
Mum is only five minutes late, but to
Jerome it seems like ages, and he has all
sorts of wild fantasies about what has
happened to her. Has she been held up,
or squashed by an elephant?
Age 4+

My Big Brother JJ
by Odette Elliott

It is the half term holiday, but JJ and
Jasmine's Mum has to go to work. JJ is
in charge. He thinks of lots of fun things
for him and Jasmine to do every day.
On the last day they decide to make
something for Mum. Will it work?
Age 4+

Books for readers of *Sammy Goes Flying*:

Why Can't I Play?
Danny's Adventure Bus
North American Animals
Caribbean Animals
South African Animals
And Me!
Purrfect!
Choices, Choices…
What Will I Be?
A Safe Place
The Night the Lights Went Out
I Don't Eat Toothpaste Anymore

Books for when they get a little older:

The Day the Rains Fell
Ella Moves House
The Silence Seeker
Siddharth and Rinki
Amina and the Shell
All My Friends
Big Eyes, Scary Voice
Dave and the Tooth Fairy
The Feather
Yohance and the Dinosaurs

If you would like to see the rest of our list,
please visit our website
www.**tamarindbooks**.co.uk